The Emperor's New Clothes

This edition first published in 2007 by
Sea-to-Sea Publications
1980 Lookout Drive
North Mankato
Minnesota 56003

Printed in China

Library of Congress Cataloging-in-Publication Data
Wallace, Karen.
  The emperor's new clothes / retold by Karen Wallace; illustrated by François Hall.
    p. cm. -- (First fairy tales)
  Summary: Two rascals sell a vain emperor an invisible suit of clothes.
  ISBN-13: 978-1-59771-071-8
  [1. Fairy tales.] I. Hall, François, ill. II. Andersen, H.C. (Hans Christian), 1805-1875. Kejserens nye
  klæder. III. Title. IV. Series.

PZ8.W1727Emp 2006
[E]--dc22

2005058531

9 8 7 6 5 4 3 2

Published by arrangement with the Watts Publishing Group Ltd, London

Series Editor: Jackie Hamley
Series Advisor: Linda Gambrell, Dr. Barrie Wade
Series Designer: Peter Scoulding

The Emperor's New Clothes

Retold by Karen Wallace

Illustrated by François Hall

SEA-TO-SEA

Mankato Collingwood London

Once there lived an
emperor who loved
expensive clothes.

Two men decided to cheat him. "We can make you some special cloth.

It's so special that stupid people cannot see it," they said.

The emperor gave the two
cheats lots of money and
gold thread to make the
special cloth.

Soon, the emperor came to
visit the cheats' workshop.
The cheats pretended to
show the emperor his cloth.

But, of course, he could see
nothing! He thought people
would call him stupid, so he
said: "What beautiful cloth!"

His courtiers couldn't see
the cloth either. But no
one wanted to look stupid.

So they all said: "Emperor, this is the most beautiful cloth ever made!"

"Make me some new clothes by tomorrow," said the emperor. "I will wear them for the procession!"

14

The cheats pretended to
cut the cloth with scissors.

Then they pretended to
sew the pieces together.

The emperor stood
in front of a mirror.
"Here are your trousers
and coat," said the cheats.
"They are so light, you
will not feel them."

19

The cheats pretended to
help the emperor dress.

The emperor pretended he could see his new clothes.

Everyone stared as the emperor walked at the front of the procession.

But they all pretended
they could see his
new clothes.

Suddenly, a little boy shouted: "The emperor has no clothes on!"

Everyone started to laugh.
"Look at the emperor!
He isn't wearing
any clothes!"

The emperor knew it
was true, but what
could he do?

He had to finish the
procession with no
clothes on!

And the cheats quickly left town with their bags full of money and gold thread!

If you have enjoyed this First Fairy Tale, why not try another one? There are six books in the series:

978-1-59771-071-8

978-1-59771-075-6

978-1-59771-072-5

978-1-59771-076-3

978-1-59771-073-2

978-1-59771-074-9

MG   3/07